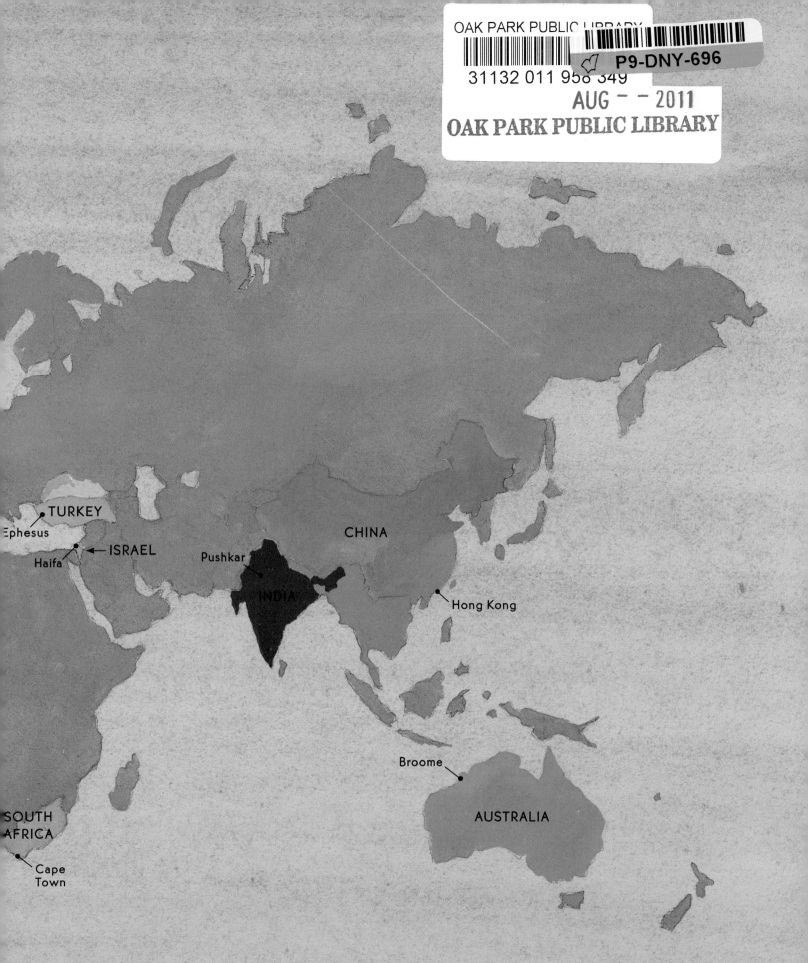

To my friend and co-host of the Poetry Blast, Barbara Genco —M.S.

For my nieces, Abigail Cairns and Charlotte Dukes, always with love —J.C.

A FULL MOON IS RISING

poems by MARILYN SINGER

pictures by JULIA CAIRNS

Lee & Low Books Inc. | New York

ACKNOWLEDGMENTS

Thanks to Steve Aronson, Shawn Davis, Rebecca Kai Dotlich, Susan Pearson, earth science teacher Sara Schenker,

my wonderful editor Louise May, and the great folks at Lee & Low.

LEE & LOW BOOKS Inc., 95 Madison Avenue, New York, NY 10016 · leeandlow.com

Manufactured in Singapore by Tien Wah Press, March 2011

Book design by Kimi Weart · Book production by The Kids at Our House · The text is set in Martin Gothic · The illustrations are rendered in watercolor

10 9 8 7 6 5 4 3 2 1

First Edition

Library of Congress Cataloging-in-Publication Data

Singer, Marilyn.

A full moon is rising : poems by Marilyn Singer ; pictures by Julia Cairns. — 1st ed.

p. cm.

ISBN 978-1-60060-364-8 (hardcover : alk. paper)

1. Moon—Juvenile poetry. I. Cairns, Julia. II. Title.

PS3569.I546F85 2011   811'.54—dc22   2010034693

AUTHOR'S SOURCES

MOON ASTRONOMY AND SUPERSTITION

Brueton, Diana. *Many Moons.* New York: Simon & Schuster, 1991.

Carroll, Robert T. "Full moon and lunar effects." *The Skeptic's Dictionary.* Last updated July 30, 2010. http://skepdic.com/fullmoon.html.

Kriebel, Matthew. "Urban Astronomy—Seeing the Skies in Light Polluted Areas." Ezine Articles, September 4, 2008. http://ezinearticles.com/?Urban-Astronomy—Seeing-the-Skies-in-Light-Polluted-Areas&id=1468200.

Miles, Kathy. "Moon Watching." Starry Skies.com. http://starryskies.com/The_sky/events/lunar-2003/moonwatching.html.

Moon Connection.com. http://www.moonconnection.com/.

Phillips, Dr. Tony. "Watch Out for the Harvest Moon." NASA, September 16, 2005. Last updated April 5, 2010. http://science.nasa.gov/science-news/science-at-nasa/2000/ast11sep_2/.

Ptak, Andy, and Gail Rohrback. "Ask an Astrophysicist." NASA Goddard Space Flight Center. Last updated August 16, 2010. http://imagine.gsfc.nasa.gov/docs/ask_astro/ask_an_astronomer.html.

Simon, Seymour. *The Moon.* New York: Simon & Schuster, 2003.

LUNAR FESTIVALS

Fitzgerald, Waverly. *School of the Seasons.* http://www.schooloftheseasons.com/.

"Harvest Festivals from Around the World." Harvest Festivals.net. http://www.harvestfestivals.net/harvestfestivals.htm.

"Mid-Autumn Festival." China Voc.com. http://www.chinavoc.com/festivals/Midautumn.htm.

"Pushkar Fair." Pushkar: The Sacred Place. http://www.pushkar-camel-fair.com/pushkar-fair.html.

Rich, Tracey R. "Sukkot." Judaism 101. http://www.jewfaq.org/holiday5.htm.

"Sukkah." *Wikipedia.* Last modified August 14, 2010. http://en.wikipedia.org/wiki/Sukkah.

Yiu, Julian. "Mid-Autumn Festival: An Introduction." China the Beautiful. http://www.chinapage.com/Moon/moon-intro.html.

LUNAR ECLIPSE AND MOON ILLUSIONS

Davis, Shawn. "Letters From Mali: Bringing Back the Moon." Peace Corps: Paul D. Coverdell Worldwise Schools, November 1996. http://www.peacecorps.gov/wws/stories/stories.cfm?psid=99.

McCready, Don. "The Moon Illusion Explained." University of Wisconsin-Whitewater. Revised November 10, 2004. http://facstaff.uww.edu/mccreadd/.

Phillips, Dr. Tony. "Solstice Moon Illusion." NASA, June 16, 2008. Last updated April 5, 2010. http://science.nasa.gov/science-news/science-at-nasa/2008/16jun_moonillusion/.

———. "Summer Moon Illusion." NASA, June, 20, 2005. Last updated November 30, 2007. http://www.nasa.gov/vision/universe/watchtheskies/20jun_moonillusion.html.

Rivera, Larry. "Staircase to the Moon." About.com: Australia/New Zealand Travel. http://goaustralia.about.com/od/wa/ss/staircase-to-the-moon.htm.

TIDES AND THE BAY OF FUNDY

Cooley, Keith. "Moon Tides: How the Moon Affects Ocean Tides." Keith's Moon Page, 2002. http://home.hiwaay.net/~krcool/Astro/moon/moontides/.

Ferguson, George. "Highest Tides: The Tides." Bay of Fundy.com. http://www.bayoffundy.com/tides.aspx.

"What causes high tide and low tide? Why are there two tides each day?" How Stuff Works. http://science.howstuffworks.com/environmental/earth/geophysics/tide-cause.htm.

CORAL SPAWNING AND BIRD MIGRATION

Lincoln, Frederick C. "Migration of Birds, Circular 16." U.S. Fish and Wildlife Service, 1935. Revised 1979 by Steven R. Peterson, revised 1998 by John L. Zimmerman. http://www.fws.gov/birds/documents/MigrationofBirdsCircular.pdf.

"Moon-Watching: Studying Birds that Migrate." Chipper Woods Bird Observatory. http://www.wbu.com/chipperwoods/photos/moon.htm.

Reefcare Foundation, Coral Spawning. http://www.reefcare.org/.

The Nature Writers of Texas Blog; "Bird Migration Is An Amazing Event," blog entry by Ro Wauer, April 13, 2003. http://texasnature.blogspot.com/2003/04/bird-migration-is-amazing-event-ro.html.

TEMPLE OF ARTEMIS

Hayes, Holly. "Artemis of Ephesus (Ephesian Artemis)." Sacred Destinations, June 2007. http://www.sacred-destinations.com/turkey/ephesus-artemis.htm.

"Temple of Artemis." Kusadasi.biz. http://www.kusadasi.biz/historical-places/temple-of-artemis.html.

GARAVITO'S CRATER

Astronomy Radar Blog; "The lunar crater of Julio Garavito Armero," blog entry by Thilo Hanisch Luque, February 24, 2010. http://astroradar.blogspot.com/2010/02/lunar-crater-of-julio-garavito-armero.html.

Today in Astronomy Blog; "January 5: Julio Garavito Armero," blog entry by Lunar Mark, January 5, 2009. http://todayinastronomy.blogspot.com/2009/01/january-5-julio-garavito-armero.html.

PHOBOS / MARS

Knight, J. D. "Phobos." Sea and Sky: The Sky. http://www.seasky.org/solar-system/mars-phobos.html.

New Moon | Waxing Crescent | First Quarter | Waxing Gibbous | Full Moon | Waning Gibbous | Third Quarter | Waning Crescent

Our earth has just one moon, its only natural satellite. Cold, dusty, rocky, and dry, the moon is, on average, nearly 240,000 miles (approximately 384,000 kilometers) from us. It does not give off its own light. What we see as lunar light is really sunlight reflecting off the moon's surface. It takes twenty-eight days for the moon to orbit the earth. As it orbits, the moon's angle changes in relation to the earth and the sun, and we see its different phases: new moon (dark phase), waxing crescent, first quarter, waxing gibbous, full moon, waning gibbous, third quarter, waning crescent, and back to new.

All around the world, people and other living things are affected by the changing phases of the moon. But perhaps the most celebrated phase is the full moon. Sailors set out to sea on the high tides it causes. Insects and migrating birds are guided by its brilliant light. Families dance, sing, and feast at full moon festivals, while traders buy and sell camels. Corals reproduce, wolves howl, and children dream of being astronauts on full moon nights.

So come along on a lunar journey to see the many ways we welcome our wondrous full moon.

New Moon | Waxing Crescent | First Quarter | Waxing Gibbous | Full Moon | Waning Gibbous | Third Quarter | Waning Crescent

Broadway Moon

New York City, USA

It waits behind skyscrapers,
a brilliant actor in the wings,
ready for its monthly debut.
On the sidewalk, an audience of one
watches and silently applauds
when it grandly appears.

High Tide

Bay of Fundy, Canada

Sail on a Saturday.
Sail on a Monday.
You'll find the highest tides of all
here, in the Bay of Fundy.

Sail at a new moon.
Sail at a full.
Waters spring up to their peak
to heed the lunar pull.

One hundred billion tonnes of water
in and out the bay.
One hundred billion tonnes of water
two times every day.

Sail in December
or sail in June.
Set out on a high tide.
Always thank the moon.

The Temple of Artemis

Ephesus, Turkey

Once there was a goddess, a goddess of the moon,

tall, fair, full of grace.

Her name was Artemis, Lady of the Beasts.

She ran like a gazelle, hunted like a she-wolf.

How she loved the chase!

Silver spears she hurled, silver arrows she shot.

Here was her temple, a Wonder of the World.

Now just a single column stands.

See the silver moonbeams mark the spot.

Sukkot

Haifa, Israel

Come in, come in,

    daughter, son, neighbor.

Come into this sukkah,

with its canvas walls,

its leafy ceiling of palm and pine.

Come rejoice in this fair harvest,

    in the harvests long past,

        and the ones yet to come.

Here, the pomegranates are sweet,

    the grapes are sweeter,

and the vanilla white moonlight frosting us

through the fragrant roof

    is sweetest of all!

Desert Moon

The Sahara, Morocco

In this tent a boy dreams of traveling.
But it is not the familiar desert he is crossing.
It is the moon.
Astronauts less familiar with heat and dust
    have walked there.
Why not one day
    him?

Lunar Eclipse

A Village in Mali

Bang the pot, beat the drum.

Bring back the moon!

If it does not return,

this bad moon will take the sun.

Then there will be neither one.

Strike the pan, wail a prayer.

Bring back the moon!

See it return, slice by slice.

Nice moon, nice.

We have brought back the moon!

Moon Illusion

Cape Town, South Africa

Outside their new brick house

in the dusty township,

Mama takes in the wash and asks her children

what they learned today in school.

Her daughter grins. "I learned that nobody's sure

why the moon looks so big on the horizon."

Her son bends over and peers at the sky through his legs.

"And I learned how to shrink that moon."

"Such smart children." Mama laughs.

"Bright as the moon!"

Staircase to the Moon

Broome, Australia

Under this sea, divers find pearls,
though none as big and round
     as that jewel up high.
Its glow builds a magic staircase
     from the mudflats to the sky.
Can someone climb and pluck that gem?
Our silly little cousins
     dare themselves to try.

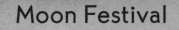

Moon Festival

Hong Kong, China

Look up!
Rabbit, dragon, butterfly, carp:
lanterns parading by.
Look around!
All of us together,
sampling these sweet cakes—
red bean and lotus paste—
each with a surprise inside:
a salty egg, round and golden
as the glorious eighth moon.

The Camel Fair

Pushkar, India

Riding high

over the valleys and hills

of camel necks and camel backs,

the enormous moon sings

    to traders, pilgrims, holy men,

    dancers, singers, vendors, shoppers,

    storytellers, and tourists alike

a lullaby to end these grand festival days.

Two children sitting just outside their tent sing along:

    Races lost, races won.

    Deals are sealed, stories spun.

    You said your prayers. You took your bath.

    You'll soon begin your homeward path.

    Bearing purses, bearing tales,

    You'll travel new or well-worn trails.

    May peace and laughter find you there—

    Till next year at the camel fair.

Harvest Time

A Farm in Iowa, USA

Every September Grandpa tells the tale
his grandfather told him,
    of reaping all this wheat
    by moonlight brighter than the headlights
    on all our combines combined.
And every year the hard-work story changes
    from old-time binders to older scythes,
    from three long nights to a longer six,
    from six strong workers to maybe ten.
But the bread, oh that bread, his grandma made?
That always stays the same!

Cloudy Night

Bogotá, Colombia

Too many clouds. Rain coming.

It's impossible to see the moon.

But she knows it's up there,

    with that special dimple.

She's seen its picture—

    Garavito crater,

named for her favorite astronomer,

    and from her country too.

She thinks, *One day they'll name a crater after me.*

She hopes, *Or better yet, a new lunar sea.*

Coral Spawning

Caribbean Sea, near Curaçao

Time to check the wet suits, flippers, goggles, tanks.
Time for the countdown rung by this fat moon.
In two days, or four, or perhaps a few more,
the sea will explode with tiny pink packets:
the coral will spawn.
Before the divers' astonished eyes,
 a crew of new reef makers
  are going to be born.

Moon Watching

Yucatán Coast, México

Flying past the moon,
flamingos silhouetted.
Two watchers keep count.

Wolf Moon

Algonquin Park, Canada

Ah-woo!

Ah-woo!

The shivering campers howl by the fire.

"Tonight, watch out for werewolves!

Pass it on!"

Woo-ah!

Woo-ah!

The real wolves warn in the silvery woods.

"Tonight, watch out for Two Legs.

Pass it on!"

Thinking About Phobos

International Space Station

Can you picture a full moon rising

    not once, but three times in one day?

He can.

Staring out the space station window

    at Earth's majestic moon,

he thinks of Phobos, Mars's misshapen satellite,

    racing, racing around the Red Planet.

One day, millions of years from now,

that crazy Martian moon will crash—*baboom!*

But till then, it'll rise and set, rise and set, rise and set.

Imagining extraterrestrials

    enjoying that show,

he throws his arms wide-open and calls,

    "Happy full Phobos to you all!"

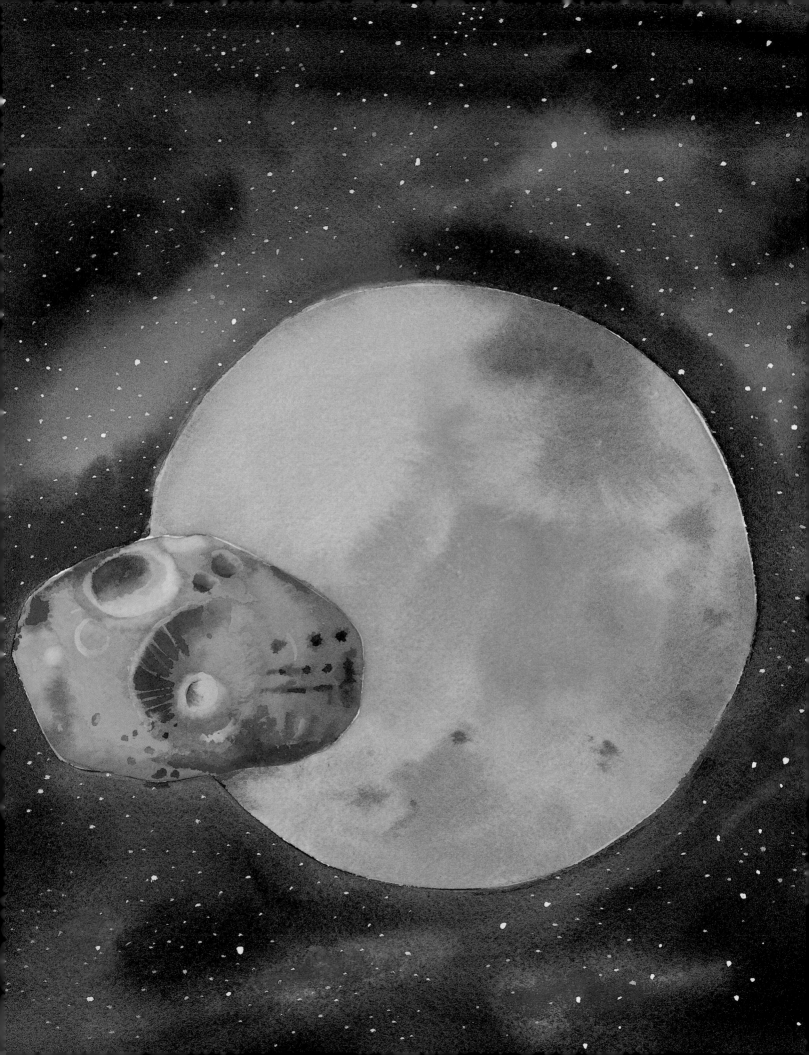

Broadway Moon Again

New York City, USA

On the sidewalk, the audience of one
is now ten.
"What you looking at, girl?" they ask.
"Oh, the moon," she says. "Just the moon."
But what a moon!
Between the skyscrapers, it takes a bow.
"Encore in one month!" it proclaims.
"Admission is always free."

ABOUT THE POEMS

BROADWAY MOON and BROADWAY MOON AGAIN
New York City, USA

In cities such as New York, it is sometimes hard to see—or notice—the moon, especially in the early evening. Tall buildings can block the view. In addition, people don't often look at the sky. When they do glance up, they usually focus on a brightly lit building or an electronic sign instead. Too much of this artificial light makes it difficult to view the stars. Scientists call this effect light pollution. But the moon is too bright to be affected by it. A full moon eventually rises high enough in the sky to shine down brilliantly on even the biggest, brightest city. Remember to look up!

HIGH TIDE
Bay of Fundy, Canada

Tides are the rising and falling of water caused by the moon's gravitational force on the earth's oceans. High tides occur on opposite sides of the earth when gravity pulls the water in the direction of the moon, and it also pulls the earth toward the moon, making the water bulge out. As the earth rotates, the high tides fall gradually, becoming low tides approximately six hours later. The highest and lowest tides each month occur when the moon is either full or new. That is when the earth, moon, and sun are aligned and the sun's gravitational pull is added to the moon's.

The world's highest tides are in the Bay of Fundy, Canada. More than 110 billion tons (100 billion tonnes, or metric tons) of seawater rush in and out of the bay twice daily. During a full moon, the water may rise more than 50 feet (15 meters). The bay's funnel-like shape and the rocking motion of that great amount of rushing water account for the height of the tides.

THE TEMPLE OF ARTEMIS
Ephesus, Turkey

Many cultures have lunar gods and goddesses. One of the most famous is the Greek goddess Artemis, who was known as Diana to the Romans. Artemis was the protector of women and children, and she ruled over wild animals, hunting, and the forest. At Ephesus, which is part of present-day Turkey, she was possibly also worshipped as a goddess of nature's bounty. Her temple there, one of the Seven Wonders of the Ancient World, was first built in 650 BCE. Historians say that it was made of marble and had many carved and gilded columns. Inside were fine paintings and sculptures. The temple was destroyed about three hundred years later and was rebuilt several times, but eventually it was abandoned and its marble was used for new buildings. Nothing remains of the temple today except a single column.

SUKKOT
Haifa, Israel

Traditionally, farmers harvested their crops by the light of the full moon, so there are many full moon harvest festivals held in late summer or early fall. The Jewish harvest festival is Sukkot—the Feast of Tabernacles, or Booths, which commemorates the forty years the Israelites spent wandering in the desert, living in temporary shelters. At this annual holiday, which usually occurs in September, depending on the Hebrew lunar calendar, people put up and decorate a booth called a sukkah. The walls may be made of any material. However, the roof must be made of natural materials such as wood, branches, and leaves, and it is usually hung with fruit and other decorations. Families eat their meals in their sukkah, and often invite friends, neighbors, and relatives to join them.

DESERT MOON
The Sahara, Morocco

On July 20, 1969, Neil Armstrong, mission commander of Apollo 11, was the first person to walk on the moon. He was followed twenty minutes later by Edwin "Buzz" Aldrin. The two men spent two and a half hours exploring the lunar surface while Michael Collins remained in orbit in the command module. Since that historic day, ten more astronauts have walked on the moon, the last in 1972. At present, several countries are planning future missions and building new space vehicles to take people back to the moon. If they succeed, who will be the next person to set foot on the lunar surface?

LUNAR ECLIPSE
A Village in Mali

A lunar eclipse occurs when a full moon passes through the earth's shadow and the rays of the sun are blocked from reaching the moon's surface. The moon becomes visible again as it moves out of the earth's shadow and the sun's rays strike it. Throughout the world, there are many myths about lunar eclipses, including the idea that a dragon has eaten the moon. People fire cannons and make other loud noises so that the dragon will cough the moon back into the sky. In some villages in the African country of Mali, people believe they need to call back the moon by beating pots and drums and making noise. If they don't, the moon will not return on its own, and it will take the sun with it.

MOON ILLUSION
Cape Town, South Africa

When a full moon is low on the horizon, it looks much bigger than when it is high in the sky. This is called the Moon Illusion. Although people have been aware of this illusion for thousands of years, no one, not even scientists, is sure what causes it. You can alter this illusion and "shrink" the moon on the horizon by bending over and looking at it from between your legs. If you "pinch" the moon between your thumb and forefinger and look through the narrow opening, you can also make the moon appear smaller.

STAIRCASE TO THE MOON
Broome, Australia

Broome, in the northwestern region of Australia, is a small town famous for its pearls and for a natural phenomenon called the Staircase to the Moon. Along Broome's coast are mudflats, lands that are left bare at low tides. When a full moon shines on the exposed mudflats, it creates the image of a staircase leading up to the moon through the sky. People from all over the world visit the town to view the "staircase," which can be seen for three nights each month from March to October.

MOON FESTIVAL
Hong Kong, China

In China, and in Chinese communities around the world, the fall harvest festival is known as the Mid-Autumn Festival, or Moon Festival. It occurs on the fifteenth day of the eighth moon, or month, of the Chinese lunar calendar, when the moon is believed to be most brilliant and round. The Moon Festival is an important traditional holiday. Families gather outside at night to sky watch, light lanterns, and eat special foods, particularly moon cakes. These flaky pastries are often filled with red bean or lotus seed paste and a golden egg yolk that resembles the bright moon.

THE CAMEL FAIR
Pushkar, India

The Pushkar Camel Fair is a five-day celebration attended by more than 200,000 people and 50,000 camels. It is held around Kartik Purnima—the full moon day during the month of Kartik, which usually corresponds to October or November, depending on the Hindu lunar calendar. On this holiday, people throughout India cleanse themselves in sacred rivers and other bodies of water. At the Pushkar Fair, visitors come to bathe in the town's holy lake, as well as to race and trade camels, which are decorated with jewelry and other finery. Fairgoers also buy and sell other livestock, listen to music, watch dancers, go on rides, tell stories, and feast.

HARVEST TIME
A Farm in Iowa, USA

Before the invention of the electric lightbulb and modern farm equipment, farmers harvested grain with simple hand tools throughout the day and well into the evening by the light of a full moon. They used scythes to cut the stalks of grain close to the ground and then tied the stalks into bundles to dry. After that, farmers threshed the grain—separating the edible kernels from the dry stalks—by beating the stalks with flails. In the late nineteenth century, farmers began using mechanical devices such as reapers and binders, first drawn by horses and then by tractors. Today farmers use combines—complex machines with headlights—that cut, bind, and thresh grain in just one pass while moving over a field.

CLOUDY NIGHT
Bogotá, Colombia

Julio Garavito Armero was a Colombian mathematician, civil engineer, and astronomer who lived from 1865 to 1920. On October 3, 1970, the International Astronomical Union named a crater on the moon's far side after him. That side of the moon, which is permanently turned away from the earth, was first photographed in 1959 by the Soviet probe *Luna 3*. Nine years later, the astronauts of the Apollo 8 mission were the first people to view the crater directly. Since then the far side of the moon has been photographed many times during manned space flights and by unmanned lunar probes.

Craters are pits created by the impact of meteors or other large objects striking the moon's surface. Lunar seas are actually large, dark plains of solidified lava from ancient volcanic eruptions. Early

astronomers, mistaking these plains for bodies of water, called them *maria*, which is Latin for "seas."

CORAL SPAWNING
Caribbean Sea, near Curaçao

A single coral is a polyp—a small, tube-shaped animal that attaches itself to an underwater surface. Coral polyps typically live in colonies. Some species make hard outer cases, with the living polyps building theirs on top of dead coral cases, or skeletons, to create a reef. Around the time of the full moon from August through October, in the Caribbean Sea near the island of Curaçao, several types of corals spawn—they send into the water tiny, round, pink-colored packets containing both male and female cells. These cells fertilize cells from other packets and develop into larvae. Some of the larvae survive to become polyps that attach themselves to rocks or other material on the ocean floor to begin a new reef.

MOON WATCHING
Yucatán Coast, México

Many birds travel in spring and fall to regions where food is more abundant. They migrate along routes called flyways, which are usually marked by specific physical features such as a seacoast, a mountain range, a river system, or an ocean current. A broad variety of birds use the moon to guide them along these routes. Although many migrants travel by day, flamingos migrate at night, as do most small songbirds because they are safer from predators at that time. By "moon watching" on clear nights, birdwatchers can see the silhouettes of these nighttime travelers and

keep count of the species as they pass in front of the full moon.

WOLF MOON
Algonquin Park, Canada

Most cultures in the world have myths about people changing into animals. The werewolf legend is one of the most ancient and widespread. Greek mythology tells of King Lycaon, a man who was transformed into a wolf by the angry gods because he served them human flesh. A written account from medieval Germany describes a werewolf sighting and says that the creature was a sorcerer whose magic belt allowed him to become a wolf. Current legend says that to become a werewolf, a person must be bitten by one and that the change will occur during a full moon. Are there really werewolves? No, but it is fun to imagine that there are.

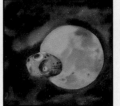

THINKING ABOUT PHOBOS
International Space Station

Mars, the fourth planet from the sun, is often called the Red Planet because of its color. Phobos, the larger of Mars's two small moons, is irregularly shaped. It orbits close to Mars's surface, racing around the Red Planet every seven and a half hours—three times in one Earth day. Phobos is a doomed moon. It is being pulled toward Mars, and in anywhere from ten million to one hundred million years, it will break up or, more likely, crash into the planet. Among the many things scientists in the International Space Station are studying is whether we earthlings will ever be able to live on Mars—and perhaps see Phobos up close.

CANADA

Algonquin Park

Iowa

Bay of Fundy

UNITED STATES
OF AMERICA

New York City

MEXICO

Yucatán
Coast

Caribbean
Sea

CURAÇAO

Bogotá

COLOMBIA

MOROCCO

Sa

MALI

N

W   E

S